Better Than Best

Books by Beverly Lewis

GIRLS ONLY (GO!)
Youth Fiction

Dreams on Ice	Follow the Dream
Only the Best	Better Than Best
A Perfect Match	Photo Perfect
Reach for the Stars	Star Status

SUMMERHILL SECRETS
Youth Fiction

Whispers Down the Lane	House of Secrets
Secret in the Willows	Echoes in the Wind
Catch a Falling Star	Hide Behind the Moon
Night of the Fireflies	Windows on the Hill
A Cry in the Dark	Shadows Beyond the Gate

HOLLY'S HEART
Youth Fiction

Best Friend, Worst Enemy	Good-Bye, Dressel Hills
Secret Summer Dreams	Straight-A Teacher
Sealed With a Kiss	No Guys Pact
The Trouble With Weddings	Little White Lies
California Crazy	Freshman Frenzy
Second-Best Friend	Mystery Letters

www.BeverlyLewis.com

GIRLS **GO** ONLY!

6

Better Than Best

BEVERLY LEWIS

BETHANY HOUSE PUBLISHERS
MINNEAPOLIS, MINNESOTA 55438

Published by Bethany House Publishers
A Ministry of Bethany Fellowship International
11400 Hampshire Avenue South
Minneapolis, Minnesota 55438
www.bethanyhouse.com

Printed in the United States of America by
Bethany Press International, Minneapolis, Minnesota 55438

Library of Congress Cataloging-in-Publication Data

Lewis, Beverly, 1949–
    Better than best / by Beverly Lewis.
       p. cm. — (Girls only (GO!) ; 6)
Summary: Filled with competition fever, Jenna and her gymnastics
teammates lose sight of their goal to work as a unit.
    ISBN 1–55661–641–4
    [1. Gymnastics—Fiction. 2. Competition (Psychology)—Fiction.
3. Friendship—Fiction. 4. Korean Americans—Fiction. 5. Christian
life—Fiction.] I. Title. II. Series.
    PZ7.L58464 Be 2000
    [Fic]—dc21
                                                            00–010395

For

Sarah Simmonds,

who gives her all to gymnastics.

AUTHOR'S NOTE

Once again, I am grateful for the help given me by my young cousin, Alissa Jones of Hutchinson, Kansas, who answered my questions about the thrilling sport of gymnastics. Thanks, Alissa, for being so resourceful!

USA Gymnastics Online also assisted my research. Their official Web site is fascinating for readers eager to know more: *www.usa-gymnastics.org*.

CHAPTER *1*

Nothing comes between gymnastics and me, thought Jenna Song. *Nothing!*

Carefully, she taped up her hands for protection before beginning her early-morning training at Alpine Aerial Gymnastics. AAG for short. During the next forty minutes, she planned to warm up her muscles. Stretching exercises were always a great way to get started before *any* sport. Aerobics came next. Last of all, individual routines. Her all-time favorites were floor exercise and the balance beam.

Keeping her focus, Jenna thought through her compulsory elements. She wouldn't allow herself to get off track and think too far ahead, even though the upcoming weekend—a three-day sports camp in Vail—was going to be *very* exciting. All week long, they had been working on individual skills, preparing for the camp.

"Hey, Jen!"

She looked up to see Cassie Peterson, a tall blond sixth grader, bounding across the gym. "Looking good, girl," Jenna said.

"We've gotta nail everything today . . . and I mean *everything*," Cassie said, grinning. She wound her long hair into a quick knot at the back of her head and stuck in a single hair clip.

"Duh!" Jenna gave her teammate a playful pat on the shoulder. "Like I don't know that."

"C'mon, I'm serious."

"And I'm *not*?" Jenna laughed. She and Cassie were both a Level Eight in gymnastics, testing for a Level Nine in a few weeks. They were also on the same All-Around Team.

"Coupled in competition," Coach Kim liked to say about the girls.

Cassie tilted her head, then shook out her arms, rotating her shoulders and neck. "Heard the rumor yet?"

"Which is?" Jena studied Cassie's face. Something was up.

Cassie leaned closer, whispering, "There's this guy—an elite gymnast—who's going to be a spotter for our All-Around Team. Lara Swenson said she heard it from Coach. And . . . he's supposedly very cute."

"So what?" Jenna couldn't care less. She was team captain and starting to feel *very* annoyed with all this waste-of-time boy talk. "What *I* want to know is, are *you* set for the weekend sports camp?"

Cassie was in her face with more news. "Listen, Jen, this guy's not just *any* male. Lara says he's so gorgeous you'll drop your teeth."

Jenna leaned down and touched her toes. Then again, this time with her hands flat on the floor. "Bottom line: If he's gonna be a spotter, he'd better know what he's doing."

"I'm sure he does, especially if Coach Kim's paying him to do it."

Jenna didn't care to respond to Cassie's comment. "By the way, cute is way overrated. And if I *do* drop my teeth, I'll just have to gum my fruit leather. Won't I?"

Cassie laughed softly. "Spoken like a true team captain. Way to go, girl."

Jenna nodded, feeling better. Finally she'd gotten Cassie's attention off the new boy's physical appearance and on what really counted in their world of competition and mastery of athletic skills. "You said he's a good gymnast, right?" she asked again.

"That's the word around the gym."

"Then he should know how to spot" was all she said.

"Later, Jen." Cassie turned and waved, doing repetitious handsprings across the soft crash pads.

Looking around, Jenna expected to see Coach Kim and his Russian-born wife, Tasya, nearby. Sure enough, the famous twosome were working with Lara Swenson on the balance beam. True professionals, Coach and Tasya were assisting all of them along the path to the Olympics.

Not waiting another second, Jenna blew her whistle, the signal to her seven teammates. Major work had to be done before sports camp this Friday. "Let's get cracking!" she called out, clapping her hands.

Once the girls were gathered on the mats, she began to call out their regular stretching routine. Fifteen long stretches total. She, Cassie, Lara, and the others were a cluster of blue, yellow, and pink warm-up suits. Tall water bottles were lined up, each marked with the individual team member's name.

Soft crash pads were scattered in various sections of the gym. Gymnasts in different levels trained on the uneven parallel bars, the balance beam, and the vault. The large padded carpet in the center of the gym was used for the floor exercise.

Across the expansive gym, Coach Kim and Tasya were busy talking with a tall, slender guy. Their faces were animated, eyes bright as always.

She noticed the young man's confident stance. How could she miss it? He had that totally self-assured look. His hair was the color of corn, and his eyes . . . Well, she wasn't much for blue eyes, she decided on the spot.

Cassie was right. He was drop-dead gorgeous.

But so what? There were plenty of cute boys in their town of Alpine Lake, situated in the middle of the Colorado Rocky Mountains.

"Stretch and . . . *hold*," Jenna called out the last three long extensions.

She and her teammates would train individually, and as hard as possible. And nothing, not even a cute guy, was going to mess up their concentration!

CHAPTER 2

"Mom, I'm home!" Jenna dropped her gym bag near the door.

The three-story brick house was unusually quiet. By now, her adopted baby brother, Jonathan Bryan, would come crawling across the carpet toward her. He would probably be drooling, too, and babbling jumbled-up syllables.

"Anybody home?" she called, heading for the kitchen.

But the counters were washed clean. No dirty dishes in the sink. The place was spotless.

This is too weird, she thought. *Mom's always home*.

Thinking her mother might be busy upstairs with Jonathan, Jenna scurried in the direction of the steps. "Mom, are you up there?" She asked this in Korean, her first language.

Mom didn't respond. So Jenna hurried to the former

guest room, which had been transformed into a nursery for tiny Jon. The room was small but light and airy, decorated in soft shades of yellow and green with white wicker accents. The sweetest nursery ever.

Sighing, she sat on the wicker rocker and leaned back. "Where could they be?" Jenna whispered, feeling drowsy.

Her day had been hectic, working out at the gym before *and* after school. These days, her schedule was exhausting. Up before dawn, early breakfast, rush to the gym, then to school, back to either ballet or the gym. Race like crazy all day long. She knew if she couldn't handle the mental strain, the stress, her own emotions, all of that, she would never attain the success she longed for. At the moment, her goal was to become a member of the Junior National Team.

Getting up, she went to the crib and leaned on the ruffled crib bumpers. She smoothed the folded baby quilt at the bottom. Restless, she reached for the cow-jumped-over-the-moon lamp on the bureau and went to sit again in the rocker. She stared at the lamp, very glad to have the support of both her parents. Coach Kim and Tasya were also two of her biggest fans.

And there was the very cool, very exciting Girls Only club. The other three members were also her closest friends—Livvy Hudson, Heather Bock, and Miranda Garcia. They liked to perform ballets and elaborate dramas for their parents. They also offered enthusiasm and encouragement to Jenna and to one another.

Jenna sometimes wondered how she'd ever managed before the club was created last fall. Livvy was an amazing novice-level figure skater, and Heather was a dazzling, award-winning ice dancer with her brother, Kevin. Manda, their newest member, was a stunning and daring downhill skier. Four girls following a strenuous, yet thrilling, track to the Olympics. They shared athletic dreams and goals, forming a tight-knit friendship.

Jenna's All-Around teammates were cool, too. They worked well individually and as a team. But she was worried about something—*someone*.

Lara Swenson, the youngest of the seven members, had just turned eleven. In the past six weeks, she had grown really fast. Maybe too fast. Right in front of everyone's eyes, she was sprouting up like she might never stop! At the moment, she was just a hair taller than Cassie Peterson, who *had* been the tallest on the team.

Jenna could hardly believe it. Did Lara have an out-of-control pituitary gland or what? Petite Lara was no longer tiny. If she kept up her growth rate, she might end up six feet tall. Jenna worried that Lara wouldn't be able to maintain her exceptional skills as a gymnast. Which would hurt *all* the others on the team.

This week she'd noticed Lara's inability to "stick" her landings perfectly. For the first time, her performances had been less than precise. Lara was struggling for sure.

Jenna really wanted to help. But she had no idea what to do.

The phone rang, and Jenna raced down the hall to her parents' bedroom. "Song residence, Jenna speaking," she answered.

"How's life?"

It was Olivia Hudson, Jenna's best friend. "Livvy, hi! Things are going okay . . . I guess you could say."

"Well, by the sound of your voice, I'm not convinced. What's up?"

She cringed. Should she unload on Livvy?

"What *is* it, Jen? Something wrong?"

Putting the phone to her other ear, Jenna said, "I'm worried about my All-Around Team."

"Why, what's up?"

"It's just that, well . . . I think some of us might need some special attention," she said.

"Meaning what?"

Hesitating, Jen wondered what to say. "Well, I think you know how it is. One of us is having an annoying expansion."

"Speak English," Livvy laughed.

"Meaning one of us has an overactive growth gland."

"Well, *you* don't," Livvy said quickly. "Not yet, anyway."

Her friend's answer took her off guard. "You're right, I'm *not* growing."

"Then who?"

"You remember Lara Swenson?"

Livvy chuckled. "Right. The baby gymnast at AAG."

"Well, try this on for size: Lara's now the *tallest* team member. And it *just* happened."

"You sound . . . sorta jealous," Livvy said. "What's with that?"

Jen bit her lip. "I guess I'm afraid *I* won't grow anymore at all. Maybe I'll stay this small—this short—for the rest of my life."

"Being petite is a good thing for gymnasts, isn't it?" Liv asked.

"So everyone says."

"Then it must be true."

Leave it to Livvy to turn things around, to try to encourage her. Livvy had always been good in the cheering-up department. She'd been Jen's good friend for a long time. They'd started out as pen pals—the snail-mail kind. Then they'd both moved to Alpine Lake with their families before school started last August. Just in time for sixth grade at Alpine Lake Middle School.

"You know what?" Jenna changed the subject. "We've got a new guy helping with the team."

"A guy? You must be kidding." Livvy sounded shocked. "Who is it?"

Jenna had to smile. "His name is Nels Ansgar."

"Sounds Norwegian."

"Might be," replied Jenna.

Livvy was silent for a moment, then continued. "So . . . what's Nels got to do with Lara's growth spurt?"

Jenna sighed. "I guess I'm not making much sense.

Nothing really. It's just that Lara's shooting up. Way up. And I'm trapped in pre-puberty."

Livvy was laughing. "Don't go morbid on me."

"I'm not . . . *okay*." Jenna felt angry and didn't know why.

"Hey, did I say something wrong?" They were silent for a moment, then Livvy asked, "Are you worried? About your height, I mean . . . because of this guy?"

"Sorta." Jenna shrugged, even though Livvy couldn't see her.

"Don't worry. He's just a spotter. It's no big deal."

Maybe not for you, Jen thought.

Just then she heard her mother returning home. "I better get going," she said, adding a hurried "Bye, Livvy."

"Call me later tonight."

Jenna had tons of homework. "Maybe we'd better talk at school tomorrow instead."

"Okay. I'll meet you at our locker."

"See ya, Liv."

They hung up, and Jenna rushed off to greet her mom and baby brother. "Where were you?" she asked, taking Jonathan from her mother's arms.

"We ran out to buy some more cabbage," her mother explained. "Your father's having his deacon board meeting here on Saturday. He wants me to cook up some kimchi. Lots of it."

"Sounds good."

Jenna's dad was the pastor of the Korean church in Alpine Lake. A small church in a small town. "We can grow . . .

and we will," he liked to say when discussing the prospect of attracting new Korean members and their families.

Jostling her baby brother on her hip, Jenna turned toward the kitchen window. She thought of her dad's motto: *"We can grow, and we will."* Would *she* grow? Or would she remain a teeny weeny forever?

Outside, the leaves on their trees were full and green— almost lacy-looking in the fading sunlight. Her mother's red tulips were in full bloom. She stared at the smallest of a clump of aspen trees. The tiny one seemed alone, as it stood out and away from the others.

Stroking her brother's soft head, she cooed to him in Korean. She was actually glad her mom had left the kitchen. "Why am I hung up on my size?" she whispered into baby Jonathan's ear. "What's it matter?"

But she did not breathe a word about Nels, the new spotter. Not in Korean or otherwise.

CHAPTER 3

After supper, a light rain began to fall. Soon the April shower turned into a gale of thunder and lightning.

Glancing out her window, Jenna was actually glad for the storm. The weather suited her mood, after all. Rain was the ideal climate for studying for a history test.

American history bored her silly. She would much rather be studying Korean history—her family roots. Often, during class, she had to *make* herself listen to the teacher. She struggled to keep her mind from wandering, especially with gymnastics and ballet and all the thrilling summer events coming up!

She stared at the Olympic rings flag hanging high over her desk. Why was she required to study subjects that didn't interest her? What a waste of her valuable time.

Gymnastics had always been the thing that pumped her

up. For as long as she could remember. Since before pre-school, she had been testing her balancing ability. On check-ered floors, sidewalk cracks . . . anything. Jenna was three years old when her mother signed her up for the Tumble Tots.

She was tapping her pen on the desk top when Mom peered in the open bedroom door. "I don't mean to interrupt, but—"

"Anytime you see this book, feel free," Jenna said, waving the history text book in the air. "And I'm *not* kidding."

Mom grinned. "Just remember: If it's not worth doing one-hundred-and-ten-percent, it's not worth doing at all." One of Mom's all-time favorite sayings.

"I'm trying, but I can't say it's any fun."

"Fun or not, you must keep up your grades."

Nothing, according to Mom, should ever be done by halves. She believed that God expected—even *required*—our best, as His children. That was her life's philosophy.

"Which leotards and warm-up suits do you want washed for the weekend?" Mom asked.

Jenna shrugged. "Doesn't matter. Just pick out two or three of each."

Mom's smile faded. "I thought you were excited about sports camp, honey."

"I doubt it'll be very cool," she complained.

"But Coach Kim is bringing in a national team coach for the occasion," Mom reminded her. "Won't *that* be exciting?"

She still had gobs of studying to do. "I'd rather not talk about it," Jenna said softly.

Mom touched her shoulder. "I'm here whenever, okay?"

Nodding, Jenna watched her mother head for her closet, pulling several leotards out of the hamper. "Thanks, Mom."

Her mother scurried out of the room, arms loaded down with laundry. "That's what mothers are for, right?"

Jenna couldn't help thinking how similar her mom and Livvy Hudson were. In many ways, they had the same intensely focused, yet happy, approach to life.

She prided herself on having a cheerful attitude. But today she had to pour her thoughts and concentration into the monotonous history questions. Tomorrow she'd be glad she had stuck it out—crammed for the test.

Mom's perspective on life rang in her ears. Doing your best affected every area of learning. Small or tall. School-work was a good training ground for becoming an Olympic athlete.

She spent the rest of the evening preparing for the dreaded test. All the while, Sasha, her prissy kitty, kept her company on the computer desk, purring as if she had not a care in the world.

"Must be nice," Jenna said, leaning her head against the golden-haired cat.

"What kept you so long?" Livvy asked the next day. She

was primping in the mirror of their shared locker. "I thought you'd never get here."

Jenna glanced at her watch. "I'm not late, am I?"

Livvy turned to look her over. "Not exactly."

"Then what?"

"We have to talk," Livvy whispered.

"About what?"

Livvy jerked her head toward the busy hall of students. "Check it out, over there."

"Should I look now?" Jenna whispered back.

"It's Nels Ansgar, the guy you told me about."

Both girls turned to gawk—discreetly, of course—at a tall boy with golden hair. He was rushing down the hall to a locker on the opposite side.

"Look, he even strides like a gymnast," Livvy remarked.

"You should see him on the uneven bars," replied Jenna. "He makes it look so easy."

"I hear he's thirteen." Livvy commented.

"That would put him in either seventh or eighth grade."

"Probably eighth," Jenna said. "He acts older, don't you think?"

"Maybe he's not enrolled here."

"Then why's he hanging out at school?"

Livvy ignored the question. "He's just so tall and . . . cute."

Everyone thinks tall is best, Jenna thought.

"Why haven't we noticed him around school before?" Livvy asked as they closed the locker.

"Maybe he's new to town."

"Are you sure?" Livvy asked, turning to look at Jenna.

"Not really. Maybe he's a foreign exchange student." She wondered about that. Maybe Nels *wasn't* a permanent fixture here in Alpine Lake. Surely Cassie or Lara would know. Coach Kim and his wife would, too. Jenna wasn't too curious or interested in sticking her neck out to get info. Not for a guy who was as tall as he was cute.

She could just imagine the ongoing distraction a team spotter like Nels might cause.

What *was* Coach thinking?

The history test was worse than Jenna anticipated. At one point she closed her eyes, trying to remember the pages she'd read last night. Why had she waited so long to study?

I need to change my game plan about American History class, she thought. *Think of it as a gymnastics meet, where it's best to train way ahead*.

Struggling through five essay questions, she decided she would begin studying tonight for the next test. What a monster of a test. Hardly any multiple-choice questions. Mostly true or false questions—the worst. You either knew it or you didn't.

She took her time, going back to check and double-check her answers. *"Iron the small things,"* Coach Kim always said. Well, she'd have to transfer what she was learning at the gym into her school studies. Especially history.

When she was finished, she sat at her desk, staring at the first page of the test. She didn't get up and turn it in right then. Instead, she prayed silently. She was sorry for putting off the studying part. She prayed she'd get a better-than-passing grade. If not, Mom and Dad would give her the third degree, asking why she'd bombed the test.

She had enough to think about without something like that!

Jenna, Cassie, and Lara worked on their aerial cartwheels for over an hour after school, following Natalie Johnston's ballet class. They were really warmed up by the time they arrived at Alpine Aerials Gym.

But Nels had other ideas about warming up. With no effort at all, he'd gathered the girls around him. They watched, nearly transfixed, as he did his pirouettes and saltos with multiple grip changes on the uneven parallel bars. His flight was definitely high. No question, Nels was a superb gymnast.

"What's this, a one-man show?" Jenna whispered to Cassie.

"He's just practicing, that's all," Cassie said flippantly.

"Showing off, don't you mean?"

"What's *your* problem?"

"Sorry I asked." Jenna turned away.

"He's adorable, isn't he?" Lara grabbed Jenna's arm.

"You've lost your focus," she shot back. As far as Jenna was concerned, Nels was hired help—here to help Coach and Tasya spot during sports camp. He would probably head back home to Europe, or wherever, after this weekend. End of story.

Both Cassie and Lara stood gazing at the new boy like he was an Olympic superstar. They were definitely flipped out.

"I don't believe this," Jenna muttered, walking toward the water fountain. "He's going to be the end of us."

"Who is?"

She turned to see Coach Kim looking up at her from his clipboard.

"Oh, uh . . . nothing," she managed to say to Coach.

"Well, now, other than myself, there's only one *male* in the gym at the moment." His wry smile gave him away.

She could kick herself. Coach had heard her mumbling about Nels Ansgar.

What could she say?

CHAPTER 4

Jenna made an attempt to explain herself to Coach Kim. But she was spared the embarrassment when the whistle blew for team warm-ups.

"Time to lead stretching exercises," Coach said. He meant for her to get moving and fill her duty as captain.

Dashing across the maze of mats and equipment, Jenna met up with the girls. But it was Nels who had *her* whistle!

"Excuse me." She put her hands on her hips. "*I'm* the team captain."

Smiling down at her, he said, "Captain Song, is it?"

"Jenna."

"Glad to meet you, Jenna Song. I'm Nels Ansgar." Grinning, he handed over the silver whistle and stepped back, behind the girls' lineup.

Jenna observed that he was only slightly taller than Lara

Swenson. His smiling blue eyes and extraordinary good looks rattled Jenna. She even forgot to wipe off the whistle before putting it to her own lips.

Warm-ups went as well as could be expected. As long as Jenna kept her eyes on either Cassie, Lara, or the other girls, she was perfectly fine. But locking eyes with Nels made her flustered.

Did the other girls feel the same way?

During floor routines, Lara stumbled a lot. She was obviously off kilter. Lara had always been well-known for super-charged, brilliant performances. Consistently perfect. She nailed everything—tumbles, acrobatics, and sequences. Every time.

Not today.

Yet Coach was patient with Lara. He and Tasya guided her repeatedly through several sequences and dance movements. "Things will improve over time. . . ." His voice trailed off.

Jenna truly felt sorry for Lara. No longer was her friend a Dominique or Nadia look-alike. She was no longer a pint-size.

And Jenna felt sorry for herself, too. She *still* had a mini, little-girl body like young Domi and Nadia. She was always first in line of all her teammates when they were arranged as stairsteps at competitions and gymnastic events. But what

Jenna wanted most was to be normal. To grow some more. To grow up . . .

What was so wrong with that?

Turning her concentration back to her floor exercise, she fought hard the urge to glance at the girls. All of them were cheering her on.

Coach Kim and Tasya had trained them to encourage one another. "Pump up your teammates," Coach liked to say. "Work as a team. Work hard at caring."

If one member stumbled, they all must feel the pain. The disappointment. Then push past the problem and succeed to perfection. They—all of them—were expected to move, breathe, and live the AAG motto: *Be your best. Be perfect.*

The motto kept her sharp, on her toes at all times.

Nels took his position as spotter.

I don't need him, she thought but wouldn't cause a scene. She would just ignore him. Pretend he wasn't there.

"Hit it, Jenna . . . hit it . . ." the All-Around Team chorused from the sidelines.

The force of their chanting, mixed with Nels' slightly lower voice, inspired her. She was ready to give the routine her best shot.

"Be your best," Cassie hollered.

I'll try for better than best, she thought. She would not miss this moment to excel.

The musical introduction to her floor exercise—"A Whole New World"—spilled out of the speakers. Jenna stared down at the square of carpet, forty feet by forty feet. She would complete each of her skills using every inch of the carpet space. And she would not allow her tiny feet to cross the line.

She saluted the imaginary judges, as she was taught to do. Both arms high over her head, she saluted as if to say, "Look at me! I'm ready to perform perfectly!"

Feeling the burst of confidence, she pointed her toes and began the dance sequence. Next came the tumbling pass. She was so jazzed, she nailed every layout, handspring, and salto. Best of all, she hit her final pose perfectly.

Coach was yelling, "You did it, Jenna! You were wonderful!" He hugged her, twirling her around.

She caught Nels' eye just then. His face was way too serious. Instead of smiling, he was frowning. While the girls clapped and cheered for her, he remained motionless and silent.

Is he jealous? she wondered.

It was starting to rain again when her dad parked in front of the gym. "How was practice?" he asked.

"Which one?" She had worked out both before school and after ballet, right after school.

"Both." He waited for her answer before turning into the street.

"Well, this afternoon I really beat the nerves," she was

proud to say. "Morning practice wasn't so hot, but that's not *my* problem."

"Oh?"

"Yeah," she muttered. "Did Mom say anything to you?"

A smile spread across his face. "Your mother says lots of things to me." He was such a tease.

"C'mon, Daddy, you know what I mean."

"Well," he said, keeping his attention on the road, "your mother hopes the weekend will be a good experience for you."

"So do I." She wouldn't say more. Mom and Dad were definitely on her side.

He glanced over at her. "You do *want* to go to Vail, don't you?"

She was quiet for a moment. "Sure, I'm planning to go."

"But. . . ?"

She remembered the way Nels had looked at her when her floor exercise was as perfect as they get. She remembered, too, how he'd blown her whistle for warm-ups. Did he want to take over her position?

"Will you miss me?" she said with confidence.

He reached over and patted her shoulder. "We'll miss you both at home and at church. Your brother will miss your hugs and all the silly baby talk."

Thinking of the baby her parents had adopted back in December, she had to smile. It seemed, nearly overnight, the little tyke had won her heart.

Becoming an extraordinary gymnast meant plenty of sacrifice. But that was part of the training. Three days away from her family might be a little unpleasant. In the end, though, the special emphasis would be worth it.

Now, if only the team would pull together. She hoped and prayed they could, in spite of Nels. She hoped the girls would pay attention to their own skills. Not be so google-eyed over the spotter.

If only Nels hadn't come to Alpine Lake. . . .

CHAPTER 5

Jenna was up and packed long before the early-morning departure. Over the past few days, she'd gotten behind in recording her thoughts in her journal.

So she wrote quickly.

Friday (5:30 A.M.), April 7
Dear Diary,
    Last night, Livvy and I talked after ballet class. She and the other Girls Only members are going to Vail for the sports camp weekend, too. I'm so jazzed! Of course, we won't be together all that much—only during the ballet segment. But we'll hang out at night in the dorm. We're planning to have a club meeting while we're there. Hope the sponsors don't mind our giggling.
    I think Cassie's head over heels about Nels, the new spotter for the All-Around Team. Lara is trying to com-

pete with Cassie for his attention. But he doesn't really seem interested in either of them. Go figure . . .

Gotta run. I hear Dad calling me to bring my luggage downstairs. One little sports bag. Won't he be surprised?

Speaking of surprises, I have a strange feeling about this weekend. But I hope I'm wrong!

Coach Kim and Tasya kept the gymnasts entertained in the van on the ride to Vail. Tasya told amusing and heart-warming tales of national competitions in Russia, and around the world.

"Our tour took us all the way to New York City," Tasya said. "Coach and I fell in love with the Big Apple. And by that time, we were quite disappointed with the Russian government for many reasons."

Jenna and her friends listened intently, eager for more of the story.

"The morning we were scheduled to fly back to Russia, Coach Kim and I spoke to the American officials." She grinned, looking fondly at Coach. "Tell them the rest, dear."

Coach glanced in the rearview mirror. "Can anyone guess what happened?" he bellowed.

Jenna raised her hand. "You stayed in America!"

"Tasya defected from Russia," said Cassie.

The whole van was cheering. "Hooray for Tasya!"

It was a thrilling moment, especially for Jenna. She felt she understood the triumph of being granted asylum because her ancestry was closely tied to another country. She, too, was proud to call herself an American citizen. It was thrilling to hear the national anthem played or sung at gymnastic events.

"On that day, we started all over with nothing," Tasya said softly when the hoopla died down. "Such hard work it was, making a new home in America. But it was worth every struggle."

Just like gymnastics, thought Jenna.

She was thinking of the effort that went into perfecting every single gesture, every movement, every breath. Flashy, impressive moves fell flat if the smallest motions were sloppy or incomplete. Bad habits had to be relearned and replaced with good ones. The overall performance was a make-or-break situation, depending on all of the above.

Within minutes of their arrival in Vail, they were registered. Then the intense training began. Physical skills were one thing, the other hurdle was the test for mental toughness. To be a successful gymnast, focusing one hundred percent was most important. Jenna knew that if one tiny detail was overlooked in any of her routines, the whole program was zip.

She was determined to master her skills—to benefit from

the three-day sports camp. No matter what.

The first three hours, she did "timers," a trick cut down—abbreviated. She raced along the vault runway and flew into a roundoff handspring. Nels was nearby, but she never once looked at him.

To get the feel of the springboard under her bare feet, she stopped abruptly, not doing the flying skill over the vault. By repeating this many times, she "made friends" with the springboard. This was the goal of the exercise.

"Doing fine?" Lara asked her during the first break.

"Yeah, how about you?"

Lara frowned, patting her own head. "Getting used to extra inches is real tough."

"It'll take time, but you're sticking with it. That's what counts." Jenna sipped some fresh carrot juice.

Lara stared at the juice in Jenna's hand. "How can you stand that stuff?"

Jenna smiled. "Well, if it didn't give me so much energy, I'd probably never drink it."

"You're saying it's an acquired taste?"

Jenna nodded, finishing off the container. "But it's easy on the stomach."

Lara laughed. "You sound like my grandpa. He's always talking about food that 'goes down easy.'"

They giggled at that.

"I'm not *that* old, thank goodness," Jenna said.

"Mom says to enjoy the strength and stamina we have now, as young gymnasts."

"Because it won't last forever?" Jen added.

Lara was nodding her head. "Sounds like your mom and mine are in cahoots."

"Actually," Jenna said, "when we're too old to perform, we can instruct other gymnasts."

"Teaching is the last thing I want to do."

Jenna tossed away her carrot juice container. "For now, all I can think of is Olympic gold. I eat it, drink it, and breathe it."

Lara agreed. "I'm with you. Getting on a national team would be so awesome, wouldn't it?" Suddenly she looked sad. "That is, *if* I can ever get control of my legs again."

Jenna put her arm around her friend. "Keep your chin up. It'll happen. You'll see."

"I'd trade places with you any day," Lara whispered, eyes glistening.

Jenna could hardly believe her ears. They linked arms and hurried back across the gym toward the vaulting horse.

Lara said, "Be thankful you're still so small."

So small . . .

Jenna didn't want to hear that about her size. She wanted to grow taller than this minibody of hers. She wanted to become a normal-sized young woman.

When would it happen?

CHAPTER 6

Jenna stared at the vaulting horse—vault for short. It stood four feet high, five feet long, and eleven inches wide. The runway, leading to the vault, was three feet wide and eighty-two feet long. She knew she'd have to be very fast, with a strong burst of energy to build up enough speed.

"You can do it!" Cassie, Lara, and the other girls called from the sidelines.

"Go, Captain Jen," a male voice called.

She saw Nels in the crowd of gymnasts. Some were from the Vail area. Others had driven from as far away as Denver and Grand Junction. Seventy-five young gymnasts, in various levels.

Coach Kim cheered her on, clapping his hands, as he stood on the sidelines. "You've got what it takes. Think 'the best.' Okay! Push for perfection!"

She faced the horse, focusing deliberately. She thought through her explosive hurdle off the springboard. Her legs must fly high over her head, toes pointed. The next move was a half twist before pushing off the horse with her hands. Her body must create a tall, perfect arc, with an assortment of bends and somersaults.

Last of all, her feet would smack the mat with a deft "stick" landing. Hops and steps backward never cut it with the judges at the competition stage. At all costs, she must avoid any hint of sloppiness in practice.

Be the best, she told herself. *Better than best.*

It was time the All-Around Team saw who was tops. She would show her stuff. She would stretch past her best, to perfection. She was so psyched up, she almost could fly!

"You were so amazing," Cassie said as she and Lara gathered around Jenna after the vault.

"Thanks, but believe it or not, I'm not that crazy about the vault," Jenna admitted.

"Could've fooled me," Lara said.

"Me too," said Nels, walking up to them.

Instantly Cassie and Lara clammed up. But Jenna wasn't going to let Nels' presence spoil her moment of victory. "What's *your* best event?" she asked him.

"Me?" He turned comically, looking behind him.

"Yes, *you.*"

"Uneven bars. What's yours?" His eyes twinkled with interest.

By revealing her best, she would be confessing her weaker skills. She glanced nervously at Cassie and Lara.

Cassie frowned. "What?" she mouthed silently.

My girl friends know the truth, she thought. Both Cassie and Lara—Coach too—knew her preferred events.

"C'mon, Captain. Cough it up." Nels' smile made her soften. Maybe telling him wasn't such a big deal, after all.

But no, something kept her back. Both the floor exercise and the balance beam were her all-time best. Her greatest passions in gymnastics. But she wanted to keep this to herself for now. She shrugged him off. "I . . . uh, later," she managed to say.

Nels looked puzzled but didn't push the question. "Whatever," he said, following the girls into the cafeteria.

They kept pace, the three of them, side by side.

"Guess who's tagging along?" Cassie whispered.

"And guess who likes *you*?" Lara teased.

Jenna smirked. "Guess who's *toast*?"

Cassie and Lara gave her confused looks, but they said no more.

Jenna had already guessed that Nels had singled her out. That he liked her. But cute or not, he was obnoxiously competitive. Not that an ambitious spirit wasn't *totally* essential for an athlete. But Nels Ansgar was a pain about it. He acted like a medalhead or something.

Jenna decided to try to throw him off, just a bit. So she

waited till Cassie and Lara were out of earshot. "You asked about my favorite event?" she taunted him.

He'd already sat down at a long table. "Sure, what is it?"

"Can you guess?"

"The beam?"

She grimaced. "It's okay, I guess."

"Floor exercise?"

She shook her head, but her heart pounded. "Floor exercise stinks."

"You're kidding, right?"

"Nope."

His eyes squinted. She had him. He could *not* figure her out. "I saw you training yesterday at the gym. Your floor routine was outstanding." He didn't crack a smile. His eyes held hers. He was testing her, she was fairly certain.

"I just give it all I've got, no matter the skill."

It was his turn to shrug her off. "Every good gymnast is *supposed* to do that."

"So what do *you* like best?" she asked.

Cassie and Lara were waving her over. Looked like they'd found a table near the juice stand.

"Well, gotta go. See ya around," she said.

"Hey, I thought—"

"Later," she interrupted.

"So long, Captain Song." There was a knowing ring in his voice. It was as if he were taunting her.

She didn't like it one bit. She resented his scoffing her name. He'd made fun of her title, too. She wished he'd stayed in his own country, far away from Colorado.

Why had Coach Kim and Tasya bothered to bring him all the way to America just for a few days of sports camp? It made no sense.

Marching toward Cassie and Lara, she was secretly glad she had tricked Nels. For all she cared, he could mistakenly think she disliked the floor exercise.

Lie or not, it served him right!

CHAPTER 7

All four Girls Only club members relaxed in the third-floor dorm above the sports center overlooking the Vail mountains. Posters of various celebrity-status sports heroes decorated the walls across the long, narrow room. There were showers and bathrooms at the opposite end of each wing, complete with hair dryers. A first!

"We survived our first day of camp," Jenna said, lying back on her bunk.

"It was hard work but lots of fun," said Livvy. She towel-dried her auburn hair as she sat on Jenna's bunk. "I'm glad ballet sessions are happening all weekend."

Jenna nodded, filing her fingernails. "If the ballet segment wasn't being offered, the Girls Only club wouldn't be meeting here tonight."

"Supercool," replied Livvy. "I'm glad we have *one* sport in common."

"Me too," Manda spoke up. She was curled up on her bunk, leaning back on two pillows. "Otherwise, I know you three wouldn't be hanging out with *me* on the ski slopes, right?"

"Hey, you can't say that," Heather insisted. Her blond hair billowed down over her shoulders. "Some of us are big risk takers. Right, Livvy?"

Livvy laughed. "Well, I'd rather not gamble with my life on ski runs like that. You're the fearless one of us, Manda."

Heather's face drooped a bit. "Really? Well, let me tell you about fearless." She began to describe in detail several new stunts she and her ice-dancing brother and partner were learning. "One wrong move, or one half inch off, and my head's crashing into the ice! Now, if that's not daring, I don't know what is."

Jenna spoke up. "You're right. Both you and Manda are the thrill seekers."

Livvy said no more. Obviously, she wasn't going to fight for a slot on the most-daring list. Not tonight.

Jenna knew what truly motivated Livvy. It was all about excelling in her sport and had nothing to do with thrills and chills. Liv had already gone through a frightening experience. Nearly one year ago, her mother had lost her battle with cancer. Jenna was positively sure her best friend was more cautious than the other club members because of her deep loss.

The official start of the Girls Only meeting began with prayer. Jenna usually prayed, but instead, she asked Livvy Hudson, the vice-president.

"Dear heavenly Father," Livvy began, "thanks for giving us the chance to come here. Help us stay focused on the things we need to learn and perfect. For your honor and glory, we pray these things. Amen."

After the prayer, Manda stared at Jenna. "What's wrong— why didn't *you* pray?" she asked, sitting cross-legged at the foot of her mattress.

"Nothing's wrong," Jenna replied quickly.

"Right," mocked Heather Bock. "You can't fool us."

Manda twisted her dark locks. "My guess? Something happened today. Something got you off on the wrong foot."

"Hopefully not one of the coaches," Heather said smugly.

All three girls were staring a hole in her. Jenna knew she'd have to level with them sooner or later. "Time for the reading of the minutes," she said, ignoring them. "Will the secretary please bring us up-to-date on last month's meeting?"

Heather's eyes widened. "I didn't bring along the minutes notebook," she confessed. "I didn't know we were having a formal club meeting."

Jenna looked at Livvy and shrugged. Manda and Heather exchanged glances and frowned.

"Maybe you could *recite* the minutes from memory," Jenna suggested.

Manda grinned. "Yeah, and we'll help fill in any holes if you forget something."

"Me, forget?" Heather joked.

"Well, there's no forgetting the Passion Play we performed last month," Livvy pointed out. "Remember that?"

Only three of the girls had been involved in the creative presentation called *Resurrection*. Manda had gone to Kansas for Easter, so she couldn't be in the play.

"Remember those quick changes we had to make, because each of us played two different parts?" said Heather.

"I thought it was supercool," Livvy said softly. "We should make it an annual event."

"Right, and next year Manda gets a lead part, okay?" Jenna said, tossing a pillow at their Hispanic friend.

"Oh, I can't wait," Manda said sarcastically. "But what I want to know right now is, what's bugging *you*, Jen?"

Scratching her head, Jenna pretended not to hear.

"C'mon, don't do that," Heather protested.

"Do what?" Jenna said, frowning.

"You know" was all Heather said.

Unexpectedly, Cassie and Lara flounced into the room. They were sharing the space in two more bunks. "Are we interrupting anything?" Lara asked.

"Not really," Jenna was quick to say.

"Oh, it's your club thing, right?" Lara said, standing taller than ever.

"Actually, I think we're finished," said Jenna. "Aren't we, girls?"

Manda was shaking her head. "Not till you answer my question, *President* Jenna. What's bugging you?"

Jenna felt the heat rise into her cheeks. "I say the meeting's adjourned."

"Okay, have it your way." Manda got up and draped her arm around Heather. She whispered something, and both girls glanced Jenna's way.

"Hey . . . no secrets," Livvy said, obviously sticking up for Jenna.

But Jenna didn't care if Manda and Heather talked behind her back. Besides, she had every right to keep her opinions to herself. No way was she going to say why she was ticked off. Mainly because she was so upset with herself.

CHAPTER 8

Jenna tossed and turned, trying to get comfortable in bed. The narrow bunk, probably a twin-size, seemed smaller than that. At least it wasn't lumpy like the mattresses at other sports camps she'd attended. Something to be thankful for!

When she finally *did* fall asleep, she dreamed she was riding bikes with Lara Swenson. The wind was in their hair as they flew over the bluffs on the outskirts of Alpine Lake.

Midway down the hill, she realized her feet didn't reach the pedals. Surprised, she saw that the bike was a minibike with training wheels!

This is crazy. I know I'm bigger than this! She panicked.

She awakened with a start and sat straight up in the bunk. The dorm was dark and still. The other girls were sound asleep. Lara Swenson was snoring. Livvy, in the next bunk, was half in, half out of bed, with one leg flung over the side.

Slowly, Jenna leaned back onto the mattress, wondering about the weird dream. Was she so worried about her size that her subconscious had kicked in with the ridiculous dream?

She decided she would try to brush it off. She would wake up in the morning and probably forget the bike dream ever happened.

Forgetting the dream is exactly what Jenna *tried* to do, except that during breakfast, she could think of nothing else. The dream about riding a beginner's bike plagued her thoughts.

Is that really how I feel about my body? she wondered. *Am I too small for who I want to be?*

"Hey, wake up, daydreamer."

Jen looked up to see Livvy sitting across the table from her. She had a fruit plate of fresh strawberries, bananas, apple slices, and a bran muffin. "You look wiped out, and the day's just starting," said Livvy. "You okay?"

"Sure," Jenna replied. "Did *you* sleep all right?"

"Sure," Liv said flatly.

The girls' gazes met and held.

"So . . . how's it feel?" Livvy said.

"What're you talking about?"

"Saying 'sure' when you don't mean it."

There was no getting around Livvy Hudson. She knew and understood Jenna through and through.

Sighing, Jenna took a long drink of her orange juice. Then she said, "I did a lousy thing."

Livvy kept her focus on Jenna, never flinching. She'd pulled her hair back into a tight ponytail, snapping on a Scrunchie. The intense look in Livvy's green eyes got Jen's attention.

"I'm a pastor's daughter. I should know better," Jenna said softly.

"Doesn't make you perfect, does it?"

"But still . . ." Jenna sighed. She really didn't want to tell Livvy what was on her mind. But knowing Livvy the way she did, she hardly had a choice.

"I think deep down you want to tell me, Jenna. C'mon, you know you can trust me."

Sure she could. Jenna knew that. But . . .

"Is this about your hang-up . . . you know, over your size?"

"Maybe."

Livvy leaned closer, nearly in her face. "Or is this about Nels, the new spotter for your team?"

Jenna thought about the peculiar dream. She remembered the way she'd deceived Nels on purpose. She thought about tiny Lara Swenson passing up Cassie Peterson in height, all in a few short weeks.

"I'm a rotten person, that's all," she said at last.

Livvy was shaking her head. "You're *what*?"

"You heard me. I'm rotten—I lied."

"Who to?"

"Nels Ansgar."

Livvy's eyes were blinking nearly out of control. "Well, since you've confessed, maybe you could explain."

"There's nothing more to say. I just did a dumb thing."

"So . . . apologize to him, why don't you?"

She was silent. What would Nels think if she said she was sorry? He might want to know the truth.

"Jenna?" Livvy reached to touch her hand. "What's wrong?"

"I wish I knew," she blurted out, tears welling up.

"Maybe you should talk to someone," Livvy said, glancing around.

Feeling worse than ever, Jenna nodded her head. "Sure, I know who I can talk to. Besides you, Liv."

"Who?"

Jenna whispered, "My mom. She'll know what to do."

Livvy withdrew her hand. She looked hurt.

"Don't misunderstand, Liv. I just need to ask Mom something."

"Okay," Livvy said, "but if you get things figured out, will you let me know?"

Jenna smiled. What a great friend she had in Livvy. "I'll think about it," she teased.

"You *better*!" Livvy gathered up the trash from both trays and waved to her. "We've got ballet class in ten minutes."

"I'll catch up with you." She drank the rest of her juice and picked at her whole-grain toast. The bike dream loomed in her mind. Just then Lara floated past Jenna's table.

From where Jenna sat, Lara seemed to have grown another two inches or more overnight. This was too much!

She groaned and hurried out the door without speaking to Lara or anyone else. There was a public telephone in the lobby of the sports center. If she hurried, she could call home and have a quick chat before the first session of the day.

Mom won't think I'm silly, she thought. *She'll be glad I called.*

Dad answered on the first ring. "Your mother's busy with Jonathan," he said. "Shall I call her to the phone?"

"No, Daddy, just tell her I was checking in."

"Having a great time?" he asked.

She told him about the national team coach. "Ever hear of Sandy Williamson?"

"Male or female?" Dad asked.

"Sandy's a man, and he's one terrific coach."

"I'm sure if Coach Kim chose him for this camp, you're in excellent hands." Dad had lots of confidence in Coach Kim and Tasya. He had interviewed them extensively before enrolling Jenna.

"Okay, well, I've got to hurry off to ballet now. Tell Mom I called."

"Sure will."

"Love you both."

"We love *you*, kiddo."

Kiddo.

The word rang in her head like a bell. She couldn't seem to shake free of it.

First Lara, then the dream. Now this!

CHAPTER 9

Saturday afternoon, April 8
Dear Diary,

I almost didn't bring my journal to sports camp, but now I'm glad I did. To start off the day, Livvy gave me an earful about what I ought to do. She knows me as well as if she were my sister, I think.

I told Livvy the truth, that I lied to Nels. But something's keeping me from wanting to apologize. And I backed out and couldn't ask Dad to get Mom on the phone.

What's my problem?

Why am I so focused on what I'm not (tall) more than WHO I am (a first-rate gymnast)? Why can't I stop playing games with myself?

All my Girls Only friends know something's bugging me. Cassie and Lara, too. If I could just get my head screwed on, I could work this out.

Oh, I almost forgot. Nels ate lunch at my table at noon. I'm trying not to let him distract me. It's hard because he's always hanging around.

Ballet is very cool. Natalie Johnston's here, working with a group of us. Some of the gymnasts haven't had as much ballet background as I do. I'm glad Mom and Dad got me started early. Ballet makes me a better gymnast.

I'm supposed to be resting, but I feel so jittery. Now I better hide this or my girl friends will know too much about me.

I might read this diary years from now and think that what I'm going to write next is weird. But I don't care—I really miss my cat, Sasha. She's such a prissy creature, but I relate to her very precise movements. The way she walks across the windowsill is so poised and graceful. I think she has the same perfection hang-ups I do.

Thirty minutes till floor-exercise training! I wonder if Nels will start to see through my lie. . . .

The pressure was on.

Coach Williamson, the national team coach, gave specific comments after watching each of the teams warm up and perform. Jenna craved excellence and wanted to learn all she could from both coaches. Tasya, who was always nearby, especially at the uneven bars or the balance beam, made help- ful corrections or whispered, "Perfection is within your reach . . . *today*."

Extra striving would go a long way toward testing to a higher level a few weeks from now. Jenna knew that well. Eventually, she hoped to win gold medals. Olympic gold. Being able to follow through and really deliver during the most intense pressure made one athlete stand out from an- other.

She wanted today to make a difference. She was deter- mined to do whatever it took to get noticed by the national team coach.

All across the gym, there were younger girls—boys' teams, too—working out. Colorful images of leotards soared here and there. The atmosphere was charged with emotional electricity.

Cassie was in a strange mood, though, and Jenna won- dered why she seemed overly confident. A good trait to have, true. But this was very different from Cassie's usual attitude. "I adore this leotard," she said, pulling on the tight-fitting white sleeve. "I always do super well when I'm wearing it."

"Sounds superstitious," said Jenna.

"Maybe to you, but it's not really. I just like the feel of it—the way it fits me. I have my red-and-white one that's exactly like this," she said, still stroking her arm.

"Did you bring the other one along for tomorrow?"

Cassie grinned. "You bet I did."

Jenna watched Cassie work through some of the difficult

skills in her floor exercise. Then it was her turn. She was glad because waiting around sometimes made her body stiff, like it was freezing up.

Be sure to wow the coaches, Jenna told herself. *Knock their socks off!*

She prepared to take her stance on the diagonal point of the carpet. While she paced, Coach Kim and Tasya called out encouragement. "Point your toes! Reach! Focus on perfection! Okay! You can do it!"

"Looking good, Jen!" Cassie called from the sidelines.

Jenna wished Cassie, and Lara, too, wouldn't call out to her once she got this close to her performance. It was one thing for Coach and Tasya to pump her up, but somehow she resented the same from her teammates.

Except for her sudden feeling of resentment toward Cassie, Jenna felt totally confident. She was going to impress all of them. Again!

She was absolutely certain she could perform every single trick. After months of training, the skills would come easily. Like breathing.

Coach Kim picked up on her mood, cheering her on even more. "Be your best, Jenna! Show your stuff! Okay!" All the while, he clapped his big hands, grinning and nodding.

Better than best, she thought. *Show off really big today. Go, girl!*

As soon as the music began—a medley of songs from *Miss Saigon*—she was really into her routine. She and Coach Kim had listened to dozens of musical renditions of Broadway show tunes. Everything from *Music Man* to *Phantom of the Opera*. But during the first hearing of the assortment of songs, Jenna knew she'd found what she was looking for.

Her routine began with a sequence of dances, choreographed flawlessly to the music. The program was only eighty seconds long. During that time, every shade and emotion in the music was translated into leg and arm movements. Even her neck and head were involved. Every muscle strained to respond, as she had drilled repeatedly hundreds and hundreds of times. Second nature by now. No problem.

The dance shifted seamlessly into a tumbling pass. Jenna loved to fly from one end of the carpet to the other, using saltos and front full twists, roundoffs and front walkovers. Spinning and turning was everything. She was glad there were four more required acrobatic passes in her program.

Unexpectedly, on the second tumbling pass, one foot stepped off the mat. She lost her height and distance on the third pass. Sloppy—the most despised word in a gymnast's vocabulary!

From then on, her scope and distance were way off. With things falling apart, it was no wonder her landing was less than perfect. She fumbled and nearly forgot to salute at the end.

Disappointed, she wanted to crawl under the carpet. Coach Kim and Tasya were right there, consoling her, encouraging her to try harder. "You'll do better next time."

Out of the corner of her eye, she saw Nels. He hadn't

been her spotter this program. She hadn't needed one. Not for safety purposes, at least.

Looking away, she hid her emotions. She couldn't bear for him to see her frustration. Angry at her performance, yes, but upset about more than that.

Nels probably *believed* her lie for sure now.

She was convinced of one thing. Her lousy performance was her own fault. She'd set herself up for it.

CHAPTER 10

Cassie was next. She, too, was scheduled for the floor exercise. Flaxen hair pulled back in her trademark knot, Cassie stood tall like a model. Long, slender legs, tiny waist, and square shoulders. The perfect stance.

Jenna gritted her teeth, standing on the sidelines. She ought to be rooting for her teammate, but she couldn't make herself cheer or call out upbeat remarks. Instead, she stood a few feet from the padded carpet, close to the spot where she'd stepped off, ruining her floor exercise. Where a whole string of problems, one after another, had begun.

Oh, how she had wanted to impress the coaches! Desperately, she had. But she'd *not* succeeded in getting positive attention for her skills, especially from her teammates. Worst of all, she had been sloppy.

She felt miserable—angry at herself. Sure, she'd flubbed

big time. But worse than that, she'd twisted things around to Nels Ansgar. And he'd *liked* her!

Cassie, erect and poised, saluted Coach Kim and Coach Williamson for practice. She began working through her program beautifully. The strains of violin music filled the gymnasium as Cassie ironed *all* the small things and nailed everything else.

I have a choice each day about how I will react to what happens to me, Jenna thought as she watched. But she was still ticked off about her routine, how she'd completely bombed.

She struggled emotionally over Cassie's solid perform-ance. Everything was going so well for her teammate. Jenna was actually discouraged that Cassie was doing so well. Not the best thing for the team mentality. For the team captain!

They'd strived so hard on their individual work, compet-ing against one another for weeks before camp. Now it was hard to be a close-knit team.

Think sisters, Coach would often say.

For Jenna, team sisterhood was vanishing fast. Upper-most in her mind, as she watched Cassie perform, was being the best gymnast at camp. Nothing else—and no one else—mattered.

Lara Swenson—the growth gland—was up next, after Cassie. Jenna noticed the overeager look in Lara's eyes. Until a few weeks ago, Lara had been the infant of the team. Smaller than all the others, she had a pleasant personality and winning smile. Lara had passed them up in height, but she was trying her best to put forth a team effort.

She's going to do well, too. Just like Cassie, Jenna thought, clenching her fists.

Angry tears blurred her eyes. She could scarcely see through the haze as Lara finished out her floor routine, ending it with a perfect "stick" landing.

Everyone was cheering and calling, "Lara . . . Lara. You did it! You're the best."

No, I'm the best! Jenna pondered the words so hard, she nearly blurted them out loud.

CHAPTER 11

During a snack break, Cassie caught up with Jenna. "I've never seen you perform so—"

"Badly?" Jenna interrupted.

"Uh, well, I guess you could say that." Cassie reached for a large bottle of apple juice. "So . . . what was wrong on the floor?" she asked.

"I'm having a lousy day. Isn't that what Coach always tells us?" She wanted to run away and nibble on her healthy snacks somewhere alone. But she stayed, letting Cassie pummel her with questions.

"Was your timing off? Did you anticipate what went wrong?"

"Look, do we really have to talk about this?"

Cassie pushed her bangs back and let them fall forward again. "You're mad at me, aren't you?" There was fury in her voice. "I didn't *do* anything, Jen."

"Whatever." Jenna got up and went to the water fountain. When she returned to the table, Lara and two other girls from the All-Around Team had sat down.

"What *happened* during your floor exercise?" Lara asked immediately.

"Everyone has an 'off' afternoon once in a while, right?" she shot back.

Lara and Cassie exchanged puzzled looks. The other girls did the same to each other. "That's not like you," Lara said softly. "You're always so . . . well, confident. You never excuse yourself for a bad performance."

"Nothing's changed," she muttered back.

"That's not what Nels thinks," Cassie retorted.

"Keep him out of this." She felt the anger clench her throat muscles.

Cassie's eyes were wide with astonishment. "He can't stop talking about the floor exercise you performed back at AAG. He said you were the best young woman gymnast he'd seen."

Young woman?

"That was then," she replied.

"Was your concentration off?" Cassie pushed.

"Look, I need some space, okay?" Jenna said.

Lara and Cassie exchanged scornful looks. Lara spoke up. "Something's very weird here. If you ask me, I think there's too much competition going on."

"It's called jealousy," Cassie added.

"Nobody asked you," Jenna shot back.

"Jealousy makes people do wild and crazy things," Cassie jeered. Loudly, she bit into her celery stick. "I'm with Lara on this. You're envious of your own team members, Jenna. That makes no sense."

Jenna felt she was losing it. She wouldn't sit here for another second. "Who asked either of you?"

Getting up, she marched straight for the exit without looking back. *They can't talk that way to their team captain!* she decided.

But Lara was calling after her. "What's happening, Jenna? Where are you going?"

Where *was* she going athletically . . . emotionally?

She didn't want to think about it. She didn't care anymore. Being the best was her only focus. It was more important than certain team members' petty feelings. More important than a guy spotter getting wrong information about her.

She *had* to be the best. At sports camp weekends. At Junior Nationals—when and if she made it. At anything connected with her gymnastics dreams and goals.

Rushing back to the dorm, she threw herself across her bunk, sobbing. What *had* made her mess up today?

No answers came.

She could only cry, not caring if she missed her next session. Ballet with Natalie Johnston could wait.

Livvy burst into the room. "What's wrong?" she asked. "Are you sick . . . hurt, what?"

"I'm freaking out."

Livvy waited for her to blow her nose and wash up. "I think it's time we had a long talk."

Jenna muttered, "Me too."

"But there's no time," Livvy said, glancing at the wall clock. "Rythmic ballet starts in three minutes." She smiled, brushing her hair into a ponytail. "And maybe that's a *good* thing."

Jenna sighed. "What do you mean?"

"Read my lips . . . *ballet*."

Jenna stared at the mirror. She saw a petite, bleary-eyed gymnast. "I think I know what you're trying to say."

"Fierce competition can do you in. You need a change of scenery."

"You said it," Jenna agreed. "So let's have some fun!"

Livvy laughed, and Jenna followed her out of the dorm. The sun was twinkling over the tops of the tallest Ponderosa pine trees she'd ever seen. She tried not to think about their size.

"I don't mean to bring up a sore point," Livvy said as they walked together.

"Then don't."

Livvy scrunched up her face. "Well, I think I'd better."

"What?"

"I heard Nels is coming to ballet class."

Jenna could hardly think about him without getting upset. "What for? We don't need spotters at ballet."

"He's not going as a spotter."

Jenna was confused. "Then *what*?"

Livvy draped her arm over Jenna's shoulder. "He's coming as a student."

Jenna shook her head. "Oh," she groaned, "this is just great."

What's his problem? she wondered.

CHAPTER 12

Jenna, Livvy, Heather, and Manda hung out together during most of ballet. "We could have a quick Girls Only meeting," Manda said, laughing. She wore a hot pink leotard with white stars across the bodice.

"I doubt Natalie would appreciate that," Heather said, warming up at the barre.

Natalie Johnston, their ballet and dance instructor, also coached beginner through intermediate ice skating. Her home-based studio was on Main Street in Alpine Lake, two houses down from the remodeled Victorian where Livvy, her dad, and her grandmother lived. Natalie was young and petite, with a single honey-blond French braid down the back of her head.

Jenna couldn't keep her eyes off Manda's seriously pink leotard. It reminded her of one she'd worn when she was five years old. Eons ago, it seemed. Her mother had allowed her to choose a leotard for a gymnastics event. She'd picked out the hot pink one.

Thinking back, she remembered that Mom had been the one to instill a competitive spirit in her. *"Never give up till you're the best,"* Mom had always said. She expected her daughter to give her all to the sport. Everyone who observed young Jenna in action instantly recognized her remarkable talent. So why had she messed up today, of all days?

The ballet students lined up, each putting one leg on the barre next to the wall of mirrors.

Pointing her toes, Jenna stretched, leaning her head and upper body forward. She firmly touched her forehead to her kneecap. In the mirror she caught her reflection. Not smiling as she usually would be during stretching exercises.

"Grin and bear it," Natalie liked to say.

Forcing a half smile, Jenna continued the exercise. On either side of her, Livvy and Heather gracefully extended their flexible bodies forward. Jenna caught occasional glimpses of her closest friends in the mirror. For the time being, she remained silent, concentrating, focusing. Stretching . . .

Livvy seemed deep in thought. Heather, the more bubbly of the two girls, hummed a tune from *West Side Story*.

In the far corner of the wide room, the pianist began to play classical music by Haydn. Natalie distributed "the ribbon" to each student.

Jenna was glad about *one* thing. She loved to create the

spiral look, a beautiful, twirly motion in midair. The ribbon was approximately fifteen feet in length, made of satin fabric and attached to a lightweight stick. She held the stick, swiveling the ribbon in rapid figure eights. Other motions were snakes and spirals.

Natalie reminded them that the ribbon must be "in motion at all times."

Or points can be lost at competition, Jenna remembered.

Standing at the core of their large circle, Natalie demonstrated the rotating motion for all fifteen ballet dancers. Some of them were new to this form of rhythmic ballet, with elements from both ballet and artistic gymnastics.

Jenna watched Natalie leap across the floor, twirling the long ribbon beside her.

Swoosh! With a flick of her wrist the long ribbon glimmered like a graceful wand as their instructor walked them through the simple routine.

"This exercise is not a time to show off individual skills. It is excellent practice for working together . . . as a unit," Natalie said. "Teamwork is important for both ballet and gymnastic performances."

Excellent practice . . .

Jenna was reluctant to accept the idea of teamwork at the moment. Yet it would be essential to the ballet activity they would be doing. If they were to do it well.

She took her stance, holding the stick of the ribbon securely in her right hand. Her left hand balanced her gracefully.

Jenna regarded her Girls Only friends. Livvy, Heather, and Manda seemed to be enjoying themselves. She also observed her All-Around teammates, who stood together in a row around the circumference of the circle. Cassie's jaw was tense and determined, while Lara appeared to be more relaxed.

Raising her stick, Jenna waited for the music to begin.

Natalie called out, "One . . . two . . . three . . . and four!"

And they began.

Jenna attempted to match, stay in sync with, the person to both her right and left. She kept her eyes on her own ribbon, but followed Natalie's instructions and worked at paying attention to the other ballet dancers and their movements.

But in the back of her mind, she couldn't wait to call home. When could she catch a quick phone conversation— this time with her mom? She decided she'd try again right before supper.

Near the end of the ribbon exercise, she saw Nels. He and several other boys were across the circle from her, at about the nine-o'clock position. When he caught her eye, she was startled. Was that a smile?

On second thought, she didn't want to look at him again. Not now. She didn't want to gawk, secretly or not, and end up colliding with the dancers on either side of her.

She was positive he was *not* smiling at his own success with the rhythmic gymnastic exercise. He had been grinning at her. Why?

Her thoughts flew back to their first encounter. He had been polite. Nice, really. Complimentary, too. And he'd held her whistle between his lips.

What was she thinking? She groaned audibly. Her life was gymnastics. So why was she sneaking looks at Nels?

She continued with the routine until the music slowed to a gentle *ritardando*. The grand finale came as each dancer slowly lifted the ribbon high into the air, making a fast spiral.

"That was lovely for a first practice," Natalie said. "Now, let's try it again. This time, think *stage performance*."

Jenna smiled to herself. Natalie liked to refer to show time. Of course, they wouldn't have the benefit of an audience, but Natalie had a way of getting them psyched to acquire the *feel* of a live presentation.

That's when she noticed Nels again. He *was* smiling at her. What did it mean? Did he truly like her as Lara had said?

They waited again for the musical cue from the pianist. Working through the routine, they paid closer attention to unity and the harmony of their movements than before.

When the activity was finished, Natalie seemed very pleased. "We'll do this again tomorrow. Same time, same place."

"A Sunday filled up with ballet and gymnastics will be real different," she told Livvy on the way back to the dorm.

"For me, too," said Liv. "I'm always at church on Sundays. So are you."

"I wonder how things are going at home," she let slip.

Livvy stopped walking and frowned. "Are you worried about your family?"

"No, nothing like that." Jenna wouldn't admit to being a bit homesick, even though that was nothing new for her. She often felt the sinking, half-sad feeling in the pit of her stomach when leaving home for sports events.

"Did you ever get through to your mom?" Livvy said out of the blue.

"Well, no . . ."

"Maybe you should try again."

"I might." Jenna was glad for the prodding, because she'd planned to anyway. She just didn't know how Livvy or the other girls might react if they knew she'd called home. Twice. On top of everything else, she didn't want to be pegged "Mama's girl."

Even though, deep down, she probably still was.

CHAPTER 13

Jenna dialed the operator and got through to her mom right away. "Hi," she said, glad to hear the cheerful voice.

"Honey, how is the camp?"

"Oh, you know, we're busy all the time."

"That's what your father pays for."

They exchanged small talk—what the weather was like in Alpine Lake. Unimportant stuff.

"Are you missing out on an activity by calling?"

"No, I'm ready for supper."

"Are you eating well?"

She pondered that. "Well, there's plenty of healthy food here, if that's what you mean. You'd be proud of me, Mom. I'm mostly doing the vegetarian thing. No pop or candy."

They talked about her baby brother and what he was doing. "He's getting into everything," Mom said.

"I hope he doesn't grow up too much while I'm gone." She could hardly wait to see her baby brother again. Her parents, too.

"I miss you, Mom," she said softly.

"And we miss you, too."

She wanted to bring up the lie she'd told. Get it out in the open. But each time she tried, Mom got her off track, talking about something else.

Finally she blurted, "I want you and Dad to pray about something."

"What is it?"

"Something's bugging me. No, not really something . . . *I'm* bugging me."

Mom's voice took on the soft and familiar quality, and she switched to Korean. "Your dad and I pray for you every morning."

She felt at ease enough to tell on herself. How she'd purposely led someone astray. "I lied, but the worst part is that I *still* don't want to set the record straight."

"Ask God to help you. Remember, you belong to Him."

She felt better. Comforted by her mother's words.

"How is everything else going?" Mom was more pointed now.

"Okay." Jenna looked around. There were gymnasts filing past her, moving toward the cafeteria. "I'd better get going."

"You're in Vail to learn and train," Mom reminded her.

"You don't have to worry. I'd rather train than eat."

"Don't compete against others," Mom said out of nowhere, like she knew the problem. "Compete against your-self."

Why hadn't Jenna remembered this? "That's probably the best advice I've heard all weekend," she admitted.

"Well, have a good time."

"I will, Mom. See you tomorrow."

They said good-bye and hung up.

Jenna was glad she'd made the phone call. Now, if only she could put into practice everything her mother had said. Starting with letting God help her.

You belong to Him. . . .

Talking to Mom had made a difference.

She knew she had to get past the competitive thing with Nels. Stop letting it consume her with, yes, jealousy. If she did that, then she could offer him a sincere apology. Tell him the truth about her gymnastics strengths. Possibly make friends with him.

She almost laughed. *Friends with Nels Ansgar?*

The idea seemed ridiculous at best. Impossible was more like it.

CHAPTER 14

"How'd it go with your phone call?" Livvy asked at supper before the others gathered at the table.

Jenna couldn't just announce how cool she thought her mom was. Especially with Livvy missing *her* mother these days. "I got some good advice," she replied.

Livvy's eyebrows rose high above her pretty green eyes. "Like what?"

"Wouldn't you like to know," Jenna teased. "Seriously, I'll tell you about it sometime."

Livvy would only press so far. She wasn't pushy that way. "Did you lay everything on the line for your mom?"

"Let's just say we talked about *important* things."

"Okay . . . okay, I know when to quit," Livvy said.

Jenna was relieved.

When Nels and two other guys came and sat at the girls' table, Jenna kept quiet. Tall and beautiful, Cassie and Lara could do the talking. They were the ones most interested in Nels anyway.

Things were awkward. She desperately wished she could get past her resentful feelings toward Nels. And she wished she didn't feel so out of it, compared to the other girls.

Looking up and down the table, she realized once again that she was definitely the smallest and shortest girl gymnast there.

"Hey!" Natalie Johnston called, coming over to stand behind them.

"Want to sit with us?" Heather asked, sliding over, causing a pileup on one side of her.

"Sure, why not." Natalie squeezed in between Heather and Manda. "What's everybody eating?" she asked.

"Food," Manda piped up.

"But no meat for me," Livvy said, showing off her plate of pasta and cooked veggies.

"Everyone having a good time?" Natalie asked, leaning past Heather to look down the table.

"Great!" Nels said, glancing at Jenna.

Several others responded in gleeful cheers. But Lara was the only girl who spoke up. "This is one of the best camps I've been to."

"Really?" Natalie looked surprised. "What makes this camp so special for you?"

Lara's eyes moved rapidly back and forth. "Well, I guess it just has this *feel* about it." Then she grinned at Nels and the other boys.

"What sort of feeling?" Natalie was like that. She wouldn't let you *not* finish what you started.

Lara frowned, then looked around the table. "We're like one big family, I guess."

"Is it a happy family?" Natalie asked.

Lara nodded. "Sure, why not?"

Jenna, on the other hand, was thinking the opposite. The togetherness thing, the feeling of sisterhood, for her was long gone. She was actually surprised to hear Lara express that *she* felt like a family up here in the woods.

"What's everybody else think?" Natalie persisted.

Cassie looked at Jenna. "I can't speak for anyone else, but *I'm* having a good time."

"And learning a lot," Livvy spoke up.

Manda nodded her agreement. "Fun, but hard work. It's good for us."

Natalie was looking at Jenna now. "What do you think, Jen?"

She really hated being put on the spot. "It's a cool place."

Lara frowned. "Natalie didn't ask about the place."

Spiteful feelings sprang up in her. "I *heard* what Natalie said."

The table got very quiet.

"Excuse me." Jenna stood up with her tray. She was sure everyone must be staring at her as she walked away. But she couldn't help it. The former pip-squeak who'd outgrown all the girls on the team wasn't going to corner *her*.

"Work hard at caring . . ."

Coach Kim's words stuck in her head. Jenna wished she could ignore them, and she tried. But she couldn't free her thoughts of the truth.

CHAPTER 15

Saturday evening, April 8
Dear Diary,

What a long day! I don't remember when I've felt so tired. Thank goodness Livvy's so understanding. I'm grateful for her friendship and the other Girls Only club members, too. I just wish everyone would stop asking me what's wrong—all the time!

Sure, I admit I did another dumb thing at supper tonight. But why do I have to get the third degree?

For instance, Lara asked why I hated her so much.

"Hate you?" I said. "Don't you think that's a little strong?"

She said she was pretty sure I disliked her. A lot. When I tried to change the subject, she tuned me out. She's convinced I don't like her because she's taller than me. I wasn't stupid enough to say this, but even if she was the same size as before, I'd be disgusted about her catty ways.

So . . . I'm not the most popular team captain around. Guess Mom nailed it when she said to ask God for help. How long will I wait?

Tomorrow, I'm going on a hike before dawn. I'll leave and head for the bluffs before anyone else is up. I have to be alone!

"What are you writing?" Cassie asked just as Jenna closed her diary.

"Just stuff."

"Like what?"

She wasn't going to reveal that she'd brought along her diary. That she was unloading her wrath onto the pages of an innocent-looking journal book.

Cassie sat on Jenna's bunk, staring at Jenna's diary. "Is that what I think it is?"

Jenna remembered how Cassie had called out at her when Jenna took her gymnastic stance. Prior to a routine— seconds before!

Even though Cassie probably meant well with her cheer of encouragement, it *always* rattled Jenna's nerves. "You know, I've been wanting to talk to you about something," she began.

Cassie wrinkled up her face. "Oh, please spare me this."

"No, I'm serious." She pushed her diary under her pillow. "You probably don't know it, but there's something you do that really bugs me."

Cassie pulled the clip out of her long hair. The blond locks came billowing down. She ran her fingers through the thick strands. "I'm thinking I couldn't care less, but for some strange reason, I'm still listening."

Before she got cold feet, Jenna said, "Do you have to cheer for me a split second before I perform a routine?"

There, she'd said it. What would Cassie's response be?

Cassie stood up abruptly. "You know, I'm really sick of you, Jenna Song. Why do you have to pick on everyone?"

With that, she marched out of the room.

"So much for caring," Jenna muttered.

Pulling her journal out from under the pillow, she added a P.S. to the day's entry.

> *I did my best to level with Cassie. Big mistake. She's carrying a chip on her shoulder. Or maybe she thinks I am.*
>
> *Anyway, if I could just sleep without dreaming another freaky dream, I might feel better tomorrow.*
>
> *Meanwhile, there's something I'm going to do. Premeditated mischief. Boy, will Cassie be surprised ... and mad!*

She couldn't stop thinking about the way Cassie had lashed out at her. Because the dorm room was free of girls, she knew now was her chance. In one fell swoop, she could get even with Cassie Peterson.

Darting past several bunks, she located Cassie's suitcase. There, neatly folded in the back, Jenna found the sleek red-

and-white leotard. Cassie's precious leotard.

"I always do super well when I'm wearing this," Cassie had told her smugly.

"Let's see just how well you do tomorrow," Jenna whispered, removing the one-piece garment.

Hurrying back to her bunk, she stuffed the leotard in her own bag. She wouldn't keep it for long. It would easily reappear tomorrow afternoon before they headed back to Alpine Lake. She would hide it just long enough to teach Cassie a lesson in respect. Let her act all huffy when Jenna wanted to share out of a sincere heart. Sure, let Cassie be that way.

But even as Jenna put away her diary, she felt an unbearable heaviness. *Really* heavy.

CHAPTER 16

She had set her watch to play a soft tune instead of the beeping alarm. That way she could slip out of bed and watch the sunrise high on the bluffs. Without anyone knowing or stopping her.

Not a single dream had harassed her last night. At least, if there was, she didn't remember it. Just as well. She had enough on her mind.

Silently, she dressed as Lara snored lightly in the bunk nearby. She glanced at Cassie and wondered how she might freak out about the missing leotard, but, oh well, too late now. The deed was done, and Cassie would just have to endure a less-than-perfect day at the gym.

Sneaking out of the dorm was easy. She was glad for the non-squeaky doors. There were no rules about taking a walk alone. But before dawn? Well, she didn't know. But she wasn't worried. She'd stayed in this neck of the woods several times before. It wasn't hard to remember a place like this. And she had her trusty flashlight.

The air was fresh and clean as she stepped out into the predawn. Glad she'd brought her scuffed-up tennies, she sat on the porch and slipped them on, tying them quickly.

She'd seen the trailhead east of the main building, out behind the cafeteria. Stopping to get a drink at the lone water fountain, she shivered with excitement.

A brisk walk in the morning was a good thing. She'd learned this practice from her father, also an early riser. Not out of necessity, as was Jenna's schedule, but because Dad preferred getting up before the sun rose over the horizon.

"I do some of my best praying before sunrise," he'd told her on many occasions.

Maybe because half the earth is still asleep, God has more time to listen, Jenna used to think when she was younger.

As a preteen, she knew better. God was always available. Anytime, night or day. She just hadn't talked with Him much lately. Not at the Girls Only meeting. Not during her quiet time, either. In fact, instead of reading her devotional, she'd preferred to write in her diary.

Pushing ahead, up the path, she could see the slightest hint of pink in the sky. If she hurried, she could make it to the pinnacle of the hill to watch the world say "hello" to the light.

A tree branch brushed against her face. It frightened her,

but only a little. Though her pulse sped up, she kept moving forward. She wasn't really scared. Not in the least.

God is with me, she thought.

Replaying her conversation with Mom yesterday was a good thing to do right about now. What was it her mother had said? Oh yes.

"Remember, Jenna, you belong to God."

True. She knew that, with every ounce of her. She was a child of God. But her actions hadn't measured up. She had been jealous, angry, and spiteful. And more. She was sure she had displeased her heavenly Father.

Reaching the highest point of the trail, she sat on a boulder, her flashlight pointed at the ground. She looked out across the sky, to the horizon. In the distance, puffs of pinkish clouds foretold the sun's rising.

"Won't be long now," she said aloud.

Behind her, she heard rustling in the bushes.

Turning to look, she expected to see someone coming up the trail. But no one was there.

"Hello?" she called timidly at first. Then, "Who's there?"

Suddenly the small frame of a woman emerged on the crest of the path. She wasn't sure, but she thought the person might be Natalie Johnston.

"Is that you, Jenna?" called Natalie softly.

"Sure is." She moved over on the boulder, and Natalie sat down.

"Wow, what an invigorating walk up here."

"Nice, huh?"

They were quiet for a moment, then Natalie spoke again. "I saw you sneak out of the dorm. Anything wrong?"

There it was again. Someone asking her the same old question.

"I just need some time alone."

"So should I leave?" Natalie asked.

"Oh, that's all right. It's not you I'm running from."

Natalie didn't question her, and Jenna was glad. The rays of the sun began to streak upward across the deep blue of the sky. They sat in silent awe.

"God sure knows how to put on a light show," Natalie said.

Jen was surprised to hear her ballet coach talk about God that way. "My dad's probably watching the sunrise from his study right now. He's a minister and likes to read his Bible early in the morning."

"Well, it *is* Sunday morning, after all," Natalie said. "An ideal time to think—get some things squared away."

Jenna didn't respond. She wondered if Cassie and Lara had been talking to Natalie.

"Competition can be brutal. It causes hard feelings between friends, especially teammates."

Jenna sucked in some air and held it in. So Cassie and Lara *had* blabbed their complaints. "Then . . . you must know what's going on with certain people?" she asked hesi- tantly.

"I see what I see."

Natalie had admitted, in so many words, that she knew about the ongoing conflict. Jenna was actually relieved.

"What's the biggest hassle between you and the other girls?" Natalie came right out and asked.

Jenna thought about her answer. It might sound strange to say she resented Cassie and Lara for growing a few inches. "It's complicated," she said in a near whisper.

"Try me, Jen."

Taking another deep breath, Jenna considered. She wanted to tell someone the truth. Someone like Natalie, who was also *very* small in stature. "I'm afraid of something." She paused, thinking. "I really don't want to be stuck being this size my whole life."

Natalie nodded. "I understand where you're coming from. Because, you see, I'm the same size now as I was at fifteen."

Jenna worried. "You mean you didn't grow after that?"

"Not a millimeter. And I was always small to begin with." She glanced at Jenna and smiled a sympathetic smile.

Such bad news, Jenna thought. "So I'm basically the size I'm going to be? Is that what you're saying?"

Natalie shook her head. "Not necessarily."

"How will I know?"

"You won't, Jen. But one way to determine your height is to look at your own parents."

Jenna sighed. "Well, that's a problem. They're very small."

Natalie chuckled. "I know your parents, Jen, and I never think of them as short people."

"You don't?" She was shocked to hear this. "Why not?"

"Some people stand out as tall in my thinking," Natalie explained. "You don't even notice their size because they're so consistently bighearted. Know what I mean?"

Her parents *were* very generous people. Exactly as Natalie said. "Then there's a good chance I'll be about the size of my mom or dad?"

"Most likely, unless you have a very tall aunt or uncle somewhere in the family."

"All of us are fairly short."

Natalie stood up just as the sun peeked over the horizon.

Jenna joined her quickly. "I've been so jealous of Lara. Cassie too."

"Because they're taller than you?"

"Sounds lousy, I know."

Natalie went on to tell her, in great detail, how she'd had to overcome her envy toward certain tall friends. "I wanted to switch places with all of them somehow."

"That's how I feel now," she confessed. "But I don't want height to get in the way of teamwork."

"Or friendship?" Natalie said, turning to face her.

She pushed her hands into her pockets. "Friends are forever."

"Push for perfection, but don't push your friends away to get there."

"I've stepped on some toes trying to get to the top."

"You're not alone in that," Natalie said.

They shared even more openly, waiting for the full-blown sunrise. When it came, Jenna said, "Thank you for finding me up here."

Her ballet teacher and friend smiled. "I'm very glad I did."

They headed down the trail together. Jenna quickened her pace as the trailhead appeared.

"Are you late for something?" Natalie asked.

"I hope not." She was worried, wishing she hadn't taken Cassie's leotard. Jenna dashed across the lawn. Was it too late?

CHAPTER 17

The dorm was in chaos when Jenna walked in. Mattresses were upturned, suitcases were in disarray, girls were fussing.

"There's the culprit!" shouted Cassie, pointing at her.

Jenna cringed. *I'm too late*, she thought.

"You stole Cassie's leotard, didn't you?" screeched Lara.

Livvy looked on in stunned disbelief.

Before Jenna could say a word, Cassie rushed over, carrying the red-and-white leotard. She dangled it in Jenna's face. "How could you do this?"

"You . . . found it?" Jenna said, knowing.

Lara's hands were on her hips. "In your suitcase. What's with *that*?"

Cassie didn't wait for an answer. "Wait'll Coach Kim hears about this," she hissed.

Coach Kim!

This was crazy. Things were way out of control.

She could plead with Cassie not to tell Coach and Tasya. But that wouldn't help the real problem. No, the more she protested, the worse things might get.

There was only way to handle this mess. "I hid your leotard because I wanted revenge," Jenna admitted. "I wanted you to have a bad day at the gym, Cassie."

The girls gasped, staring at her.

"But I was wrong," Jenna continued. "I'm sorry."

Cassie's eyes nearly bugged out. "That's it? You're *sorry*?"

"You won't believe this, but I was on my way to return it," she said.

"That's hard to believe," Lara snipped.

Livvy stepped forward. "Stay out of it, Lara. Listen to your team captain."

Lara rolled her eyes, mumbling as she sat on a bunk. "Some rotten captain we have."

"This is between Jenna and me," Cassie said, scowling at Livvy.

Heather stood on her bunk, like she was about to conduct a meeting. "Let Jenna talk!" she shouted.

Cassie blinked and sat next to Lara. Livvy, Heather, and Manda sat down, too. All in a row, like their togetherness was meant to be moral support for Jenna.

Looking around, Jenna felt so ashamed. "I've let all of you down," she said, measuring her words.

"You go, girl," Heather whispered.

"Shh!" said Cassie.

Jenna sighed and sat on the bunk across from Cassie and Lara. She looked right at them. "More than anything, I wanted to be the best gymnast on the team. But in the process, I forgot to be the best *person*."

The dorm was quiet. No one blinked an eye.

"It's not easy admitting this, but I'm telling you straight—I shouldn't have taken your leotard, Cassie. And I shouldn't have let jealousy get to me, Lara."

Lara's face broke into a smile. "You were jealous of me?"

"You're growing and I'm not." This was tough stuff.

The atmosphere was charged. Not the way it was at a gymnastic meet. This was way different.

Cassie's eyes glistened. Some of the other girls were sniffling. Livvy, Heather, and Manda linked arms.

Brushing her tears away, Cassie stood up. "I was wrong, too, Jen," she said.

Lara's eyes widened. "You?"

Cassie looked only at Jenna. "You called it right. You accused me of yelling at a critical time—before you perform. I wanted to distract you, get your focus messed up." She put her head down. "I was jealous of you, too."

"Whoa, heavy stuff," Lara said, a glint in her eye.

"Telling it like it is makes you feel light inside," Jenna spoke up. "Nothing heavy about that."

Lara's mouth dropped open. Was she going to spout off something snippy?

Jenna hoped not.

"You're better than best, Jen. I'm not kidding." Lara surprised her, and by the looks on their faces, Lara had surprised everyone else.

"What's that supposed to mean?" Cassie said, turning and sitting on the bunk with Jenna.

"The whole team's been selfish. Anyone can see that," Lara insisted. "But Jenna's the only one who had the nerve to apologize. She isn't team captain for nothing."

Jenna was amazed at the turnaround.

"I say we team up and start caring about each other again," Lara continued.

"The way we used to," Cassie said, leaning her head on Jenna's shoulder.

"I'm in." Jenna raised her hand.

"Me too," said Lara.

"Me three," said Cassie.

Livvy, Heather, and Manda were grinning, sticking their thumbs up.

The girls spent the next fifteen minutes cleaning up the dorm room. Mattresses were replaced on the bunks, suitcases were put in order. Towels and sheets were tossed into the large hamper provided. Most of the girls packed their suitcases for the return trip home. Jenna helped Cassie straighten up her bunk and Lara's, too.

"I thought this day was going to be shot to pieces," Cassie said. "It's mind-boggling. I never thought we'd be working together like this."

Lara was quiet, but she nodded her head.

" 'Think sisters,' remember?" Jenna said.

"Boy, won't Coach be surprised!" Cassie said.

"He'll definitely see a difference in us today," Lara spoke up.

"You bet he will!" Jenna was pumped up with confidence. But there was something else she had to do. "Does anybody know anything about Nels?" she asked, knowing full well she was asking for it.

"Nels who?" Lara joked.

Jenna smiled. "Very funny. Is he a foreign exchange student or what?"

"Beats me," Cassie said. "He seems so European somehow."

"Why don't you ask him, if you're curious?" Lara said.

"Good idea," Jenna said.

The All-Around Team, as well as Livvy, Heather, and Manda, headed off to the cafeteria together. They ate breakfast and attended the early-bird ballet session.

But there was something Jenna had to do alone. Something very important. Something involving Nels Ansgar.

Dear Lord, help me pull this off!

CHAPTER 18

Ballet with Natalie Johnston was extra special today. Several times Jenna caught her eye. Then there was her occasional knowing smile.

Jenna was glad she'd gone to the bluffs. Especially because Natalie had shown up. She wasn't positively sure why her ballet coach had gone hiking in the first place. Jenna hadn't asked her that question. Yet she felt Natalie had come looking for *her*.

The sunrise experience had been a turning point. That, and the nightmare of a showdown at the dorm. Thank goodness she hadn't lost her cool and lashed out at Cassie. Her first instinct was to do just that. In the end, making peace and telling the truth was the better way.

"Better than best," Lara had said of her.

Well, she wasn't going to let that give her a big head.

There was only one reason why she had been able to pull it off. And in front of all the girls. Only one. God had helped her. Just like Mom had said.

She could hardly wait to get it all down in her journal. Tonight, for sure.

After ballet class, Nels followed her out the door. He fell into step with her. "Mind if I walk with you?"

She smiled. Typically, she might've said, "You're walking, aren't you?" But she wanted to bridge the gap of friendship, if that was possible. She wouldn't know till she tried. "Sure, let's walk," she said, not looking at him. "I was hoping we could talk."

"So was I."

His comment puzzled her. "Really?"

"Why is that surprising?" he asked.

"I thought—"

"You thought I was angry with you," he interrupted.

She nodded. "You have every right to be." They followed the narrow roadway, taking the long way to the gymnasium. "I lied to you, Nels."

"I know," he said softly.

They stopped walking and stood under a tree.

"You do?"

His smile warmed her heart. "I'm not blind, am I?" He leaned on the tree trunk. "I saw your floor exercise at my uncle's gym. You were a perfect ten."

"Thanks." This was a switch, coming from Nels.

"You're very good, Jenna."

"Wait a minute." Her breath caught in her throat. "Did you say your uncle?"

Nels ran his hand through his hair. "Coach Kim is my uncle because his brother-in-law—my father—adopted me."

This was too much information all at once. A total surprise to her. "Wow," she said. "I had no idea."

"Nobody at the gym knows, except Coach Kim and Tasya, of course."

She hardly knew what to say. "My baby brother's adopted. Adoption is very cool."

Nels grinned at her. "Someday he'll be proud to call you his sister."

"That's nice of you to say."

"I mean it, Jenna."

They walked across the wide lawn in front of the gymnasium. The sun, having risen only a few hours before, shone brilliantly. Not a single cloud in the sky. The day was exceptionally warm for April in the mountains.

"I'm sorry I deceived you," she got up the courage to say. At last. "I don't know why I didn't just tell you my best skills."

"Probably my fault for being such an odious bore."

She laughed. "The last thing you are is boring." Then she caught herself. "I mean—"

"What *do* you mean, Captain Song?"

She turned to face him. "Will you please stop calling me that?"

"Only if you'll agree to call me your friend."

This was exactly what she'd hoped for. Prayed for. But she'd never dreamed a conversation with Nels Ansgar would turn out like this.

"Call you friend? Sure, why not?"

He held the door for her as they entered the gym.

"Before I forget, my father wants to speak with you."

His father?

She was completely baffled. "What?"

"My father, Sandy Williamson, is the national team coach."

Gasping, she clutched her throat. "Coach Williamson is your dad?"

He nodded, grinning as they climbed the stairs. "Has been for ten years now."

She made the mental calculation. Nels must've been adopted around age three. Maybe that was the reason for his different last name. She rejected the urge to know. She would not ask nosy questions. "This is so unbelievable!"

"Well, you can believe it, Jenna, because my father is very impressed with you."

"With me?"

"I should let *him* tell you," Nels said, waving to her.

They headed in opposite directions. Nels to the men's locker room, and Jenna to the women's. She scarcely knew what to think. So many surprises in one morning. And such an early morning at that.

She kept the news to herself. It wouldn't be the coolest thing to blurt out this info to her teammates. Not after everything they'd just been through. And survived!

No, she wouldn't breathe a word. Not to Cassie or Lara. Not even to Livvy and the rest of the Girls Only club members. She had to hold this close to her heart for now.

Changing into her warm-up suit, she thought of her chat with Nels. He was the adopted son of the well-known national team coach. And both of them were related to Coach Kim and Tasya. Wow!

She hadn't thought to ask Nels if he was planning to stay in Alpine Lake after camp. Or if he had enrolled in school for the rest of the semester. Surely not, because school would be over in less than two months.

So many questions, yet she didn't want to pry. Maybe Nels would tell her on his own. Now that they were friends, maybe he would.

She had to make herself walk and not fly across the gym floor. Coach Williamson wanted to speak with her. His *son* had said so.

CHAPTER 19

Jenna took the lead in helping unify the team during warm-ups. Instead of taking a tough approach as captain, she decided to think of herself as an extension of the group.

Coach must've noticed. "Nice job today, Jenna," he said, wearing his AAG shirt. "By the way, Coach Williamson wants to chat with you after this next session."

She couldn't help but grin.

"Tasya and I will sit in on the meeting with you."

The meeting?

She could hardly wait. What was this all about?

Tasya demonstrated a point by hanging from the uneven parallel bars. "Tuck up very tightly to make the turn," she said, following through with a visual presentation.

Jenna watched carefully, memorizing every move Tasya made. She was eager to try the skill but waited her turn. While she did, she stood with Cassie and Lara. "How're we doing?" she aked softly.

"We're pulling together," Cassie said, wearing her red-and-white leotard.

"Yeah, we really are," Lara added.

"It's a good feeling, isn't it?" Jenna said, reaching around and hugging her teammates.

"Actually, I'm glad you stole my leotard," Cassie said.

"*Hid*, don't you mean?" said Jenna.

"Well . . . you know." Cassie grinned. "We cleared the air."

"Big time!" Lara said, laughing.

"We sure did," Jenna said. As strong a competitor as she was, she was beginning to feel like part of the team again. She would never stop comparing herself with the others. With Tasya, Kim, and the outstanding Olympic gymnasts— Nadia and Mary Lou Retton. Even with someone like Nels, who had such agility, as well as explosive movements. She wanted to observe and learn from *everyone*.

"Coach Williamson is very interested in you," Coach Kim said as she walked with him across the gym.

"I can't believe this. I'm still so young."

Coach grinned, patting her on the back. "Just wait till you hear what he has to say."

She stood in a little circle with the two coaches and Tasya, her eyes dancing. Jenna had a hard time standing still, she was so excited.

Coach Williamson had some big ideas. He wanted to help her with consistency in performance, building on her physical abilities, as well. "Jenna, I believe you have amazing potential. I can see you going very far in this sport," he told her. "You'll have to continue to work hard."

Coach Kim nodded. "Jenna never quits," he said, grinning at her. "She has nerves of steel."

"And she's the perfect size for a first-class gymnast," Tasya said.

Jenna's spirits soared. Yes, being small was very cool!

Coach Williamson continued. "On recommendation from your coach, I'd like to refer you to the University of Arizona. They're offering a terrific short-term program for gymnasts of your stature."

The way he talked, she felt tall! It was happening. Her dreams were coming true.

"I think you're much too talented not to stretch yourself, Jenna."

"And I agree," Coach Kim said as Tasya winked at her.

"Thank you very much," Jenna replied softly. But inside she was shouting for joy.

Sunday, April 9

This has to be one of the best days of my life, and it all started with a heart-to-heart talk on a hiking trail in Vail. And a view of the sunrise with my ballet coach.

Mom and Dad are so excited for me. Arizona, here I come! I'll be on my way the minute school's out in June.

Nels and I are going to be good friends, I think. He and I are much too focused on our sport for any romantic stuff. Besides, we're both too young for anything but friendship. He'll be doing some one-on-one training with his uncle and aunt—Coach Kim and Tasya. I'll see him at school, too, because he's finishing up seventh grade in Alpine Lake. It's a very small world!

My short-term goal is to shoot for the Junior Olympics. Livvy, Heather, and Manda are thrilled. So are Cassie, Lara, and the other All-Around Team members.

No more stepping on toes to get where I want to be. Life's too short to shut out friends. I'm glad I finally got my head on straight. Thank heaven—and that's the truth!

Also by Beverly Lewis

PICTURE BOOKS

Cows in the House   Annika's Secret Wish
Just Like Mama

THE CUL-DE-SAC KIDS
Children's Fiction

The Double Dabble Surprise   Tarantula Toes
The Chicken Pox Panic   Green Gravy
The Crazy Christmas Angel Mystery   Backyard Bandit Mystery
No Grown-ups Allowed   Tree House Trouble
Frog Power   The Creepy Sleep-Over
The Mystery of Case D. Luc   The Great TV Turn-Off
The Stinky Sneakers Mystery   Piggy Party
Pickle Pizza   The Granny Game
Mailbox Mania   Mystery Mutt
The Mudhole Mystery   Big Bad Beans
Fiddlesticks   The Upside-Down Day
The Crabby Cat Caper   The Midnight Mystery

ABRAM'S DAUGHTERS
Adult Fiction

The Covenant

THE HERITAGE OF LANCASTER COUNTY
Adult Fiction

The Shunning   The Confession
The Reckoning

OTHER ADULT FICTION

The Postcard
The Crossroad
The Redemption of Sarah Cain
October Song
Sanctuary*
The Sunroom

www.BeverlyLewis.com

*with David Lewis